I0635184

THEIA

DENNIS VOGEN

Dedicated to the animals

With all apologies to anyone I ever ran away from

This is a work of fiction.

Names, characters, places, and incidents either are the product of
the author's imagination or are use fictitiously. Any resemblance to
actual persons, living or dead, events, or locales is entirely coincidental.

Copyright © 2020 by Dennis Vogen

All rights reserved.

No part of this book may be reproduced or used in any manner without
written or verbal permission of the copyright owner except for the use
of quotations in a book review.

First ebook edition September 2020

First paperback edition September 2020

Book design by Dennis Vogen

ISBN 978-0-578-75932-6

Published by Dennis Vogen, Sleeping Kitty Productions
www.dennisvogen.com

TABLE OF CONTENTS

FOREWORD

This is wild.

It's August 27th, 2020, and I've just finished the first draft of Theia, which I started on August 22nd, 2020.

It's been a wild week. But it's also been a wild year, so I'm just shooting par for the course (which will be the only sports reference in this entire book). When I started this story, it was very small: I wanted to write about a silver Boston Terrier who just wanted to run away. It was, in no small part, my story – at least, a part of my story that I'm constantly at odds with.

What it ended up being was beyond anything I could imagine. It was all the feelings I've had in 2020 – the fear, anxiety, lack of control, unexpected moments of joy – lived out in detail by a bunch of animals living in a shelter.

Without giving anything away, it also ended up giving my thoughts a place to live in a way that only fantasy and science-fiction can; a safe space where literal becomes metaphor, and big ideas get small but are just as important.

This is probably my favorite thing I have ever written, and that makes me crazy.

It is as personal and universal as they come, and I can say with complete honesty I have never written something so quickly and clearly in my entire life. A week from now, I'll come back and clean this up, and shortly thereafter you will be reading these words and we'll go on this journey all over again, but this time together.

Stephen King describes story as already being there; as a writer, you're an archeologist, digging the fossil out in your own unique style. I felt like that as I tunneled through this, finding gems everywhere along the way.

I hope you find as much hope, joy and sorrow here as I felt discovering it.

CHAPTER I

All Theia wanted was to go outside.

As morning took shape, the animal shelter was more or less quiet. A whispering snore from above, a wanting whine from over there. The shelter was always entirely lit or completely dark. Right now, it was cold and deep blue, like the metal that made up their cages. All of the creatures were sleeping.

All of them except Theia.

She was wide awake. Every morning since the morning she had arrived at the shelter, she was the first one to get up. She started by aggressively licking her sleek silver coat. A Boston Terrier with that extraordinary color was rare, and her first priority was taking care of her appearance. Then she would stretch, because she knew that she would have a better chance of escaping if she was limber. On most days, if there were a bone or old toy left behind, she would sharpen her teeth on it, waiting for Nerd to arrive.

Her nose wrinkled in the air. He was late, she could smell it. She started to whimper, at first unintentionally, but then leaning into it. Before she knew it, she was growling and her voice erupted.

Yip!

"Shut up!" a coffee-colored Pitbull named Sal yelled from across the room. She was not ready to wake up, and she was most certainly not planning on participating in a prison break today.

Yip!

"Take it easy, miss," an albino ferret called Mittens said from his cage above Theia's. "There's no reason to get all fired up before you get your kibble."

Yip!

Theia did not give a shit about the other animals who shared the large room of stacked cells with her. The enclosures were shaped like a horseshoe that took up half the wall-space; the other half of the shelter had a long counter, which Nerd sat behind. There were a few chairs scattered up against the same wall that held the only door. The shelter had no windows; all the animals could see when the door opened was a gray hallway that extended left and right.

Theia started chewing on her bars, disregarding her knowledge that she would not be able to bite through them. She started scratching into the metal floor, her paws slipping in and out through the door of her cage, digging her straight to nowhere. By this time, most of the other animals were up.

"If Nerd doessssn't choke your annoying assss, I'll kill you myself," hissed a very unpleasant boa constrictor named Randy. His tongue taunted her from up high, diagonally. Theia growled with an unwavering, revving rhythm.

The door unlocked. The tension between the dog and the snake broke, and Nerd walked in, a large box under his arm. Nerd was a heavyset man who looked like a boy, and wore the same jumpsuit every day. He set the box on the counter, and turned on the light. The room collectively winced and groaned, offended by the glow.

Nerd walked behind the counter, and turned his computer on. He reached into the box and pulled out a stick of beef jerky, vacuum-wrapped in plastic. He tore at the top with his teeth, and took a bite of the dehydrated beef. Nerd chewed like an arrogant cow.

"You know I eat before you do," Nerd said to the animals. Most of the animals didn't understand many human words; humans understood nothing they said, though they more or less understood one another. He started clicking his computer things while pulling stuff out of the box: stacks of paper, more plastic-wrapped snacks and a smaller box that looked like it had been frozen.

"That'ssss mine," said Randy, his demeanor shifting with his coil.

Another person, a kind woman named Andrea, walked through the door. Theia liked Andrea, because Andrea hated Nerd, and Theia also hated Nerd. In fact, Nerd's name wasn't Nerd at all; it was Ned, but Andrea called him Nerd because, the animals believed, she found it to be funny. They didn't really understand why.

"How are the animals today?" Andrea asked, skipping any formal greeting.

"How would I know?" he snorted. "I just got here."

"Your shift should have started fifteen minutes ago, so you're late and maybe you should check that attitude, Nerd," Andrea said.

I knew he was late, Theia thought to herself.

"Get the morning report to me as soon as possible," Andrea said before she left the room.

"Get the morning report to me as soon as possible," Nerd said in a high voice, poorly mocking Andrea's. "Bitch."

Nerd took a step back to a large video monitor that hung up behind the counter and turned it on; he used this screen to play his favorite films while he worked. This was the only part of Nerd's personality that Theia liked. Nerd loved science fiction and fantasy, and so did Theia, but Nerd could die and leave the movies on and Theia would be just fine with that.

While the opening credits of *Planet of the Apes* rolled, Nerd started the task of feeding the animals breakfast. He started with the snake, because that was his favorite. He walked right up to Randy's cage; the bars were closer together for his, but wide enough to fit in a rat. Nerd put his face near the cell. Randy slithered closer, and extended his tongue to smell Nerd's meaty face. They both smiled. Nerd slid a frozen rodent from the box within a box through the gap, and Randy graciously accepted, licking his lipless jaw.

Then he went around to all the other kennels, turn by turn, and gave the animals their appropriate meals. He got their food from a large set of drawers that were up against a wall between one side of the cages and his counter. Finally, when all the other animals were fed, he grabbed a bag of kibble for Theia.

"Now, listen here, you little shit," Nerd said through a mouth that barely opened. "No funny business. You try anything, and I will not hold back on you. You understand?"

Theia didn't blink.

"Okay," Nerd said, as he slowly opened the cage.

It creaked open, slowly, and the other animals, content, watched in anticipation. He opened the bag. He poured some into her dish. The kibble came slowly. He had to give her a certain amount, an amount he would record in his morning report. The hard, dry pieces of food echoed in the pan.

Clink.

Clink.

Clink.

Theia stared stoically. She didn't break eye contact with Nerd. She wasn't moving.

The other animals started to silently speculate. Had she already given up for today? Had she given too much bark this morning to have retained any bite? The dish was filled, and Nerd slowly pulled the bag of feed out of her pen. Theia remained still.

And then Andrea came back through the door.

CHAPTER II

As soon as the door creaked loud enough for the entire room's attention to swivel towards it, Theia leaped out of her kennel. She ran under Nerd's legs like she was threading a loop; he leaned forward to try to catch her, and fell over himself onto the floor. The bag of kibble dropped and spilled over in every direction.

A Boston Terrier does not merely run. Their physical bodies simply try to keep up with their mercurial souls. There are three speeds for the breed: sloth-like stillness, a trot to express happiness or obedience, and bat out of fiery hell.

Theia was aflame.

So fast, in fact, that by the time Nerd had completely flipped over and sent the dog food flying, she was just a few feet from the door. Acting completely by instinct, Andrea shut the door as fast as she could. Theia started to slide across the waxy floor as she slowed her approach and aimed for the opening. Her front left paw had reached the threshold as she slid into the wall, and it was slammed between the door and the frame. Theia screeched like a bald tire and skidded backwards.

Her eyes said it all. Andrea looked into them and her heart broke.

"I am so sorry, Theia," she said, and got down to her knees to inspect her paw. Before Andrea could lay a hand on her, Theia sped back to her cell. Right before she reached it, Nerd wound up his arm and backhanded her across the nose. She flew into another cage next to them.

"What the hell, Nerd?" Andrea reprimanded. Nerd tried to explain that the dog was a little bitch and she didn't listen and she had it coming and as he tried to justify his violence, Andrea had walked past him and picked Theia up.

"Nerd is a bad man," Andrea said as she consoled Theia. "You did not deserve that, sweet girl." She placed Theia back in her crate, rubbed her thumb against Theia's cheek, and made a point to look Nerd in the eyes. She walked back to the counter.

"Is this the report?" she asked.

"I haven't updated Theia's information yet," he answered.

"Don't worry," she said as she picked up the clipboard with the sheets of paper. "I'll do it." And with that, she left the shelter once again.

"Stupid bitch," Nerd mumbled under his breath, so encompassed with directionless anger that he wasn't even sure who he was referring to. He grabbed a broom from next to the supply drawer and swept up the kibble, putting it back into the bag for the animals to eat later. Now that feeding was over, Nerd sat down behind the counter and continued to watch *Planet of the Apes*.

"Are you okay?" Mittens asked. His cage was two doors above hers; the cage in-between was currently empty.

"No," Theia said. "I am decidedly not."

"Can I do anything to help?" he asked.

"You can be quiet," she said. She licked her paw gently. Nothing was broken. She was sure of that as soon as she ran back from the door. But it hurt. Physically, a bit, but in her soul, quite more.

While most of her coat shimmered with silver, the front of her face looked like someone had splashed a small bucket of white paint on it, and it dribbled down to her underside. Three of her paws must have been dipped in the same paint; her back right paw was as silver as the rest. Her nose was a gray stone that rested in the wrinkles between her eyes. It was always cool and damp, and she trusted her nose with her life. Every creature in the shelter who could wear a collar did, and every collar was gold. Theia couldn't read, but she did recognize the shape of her name on a tag that hung from a ring.

Mittens's feelings were not hurt in this exchange. He understood that Theia was in pain, and he understood what she wanted. Who wouldn't want to be free? He dreamed of it sometimes, too, but hadn't thought of a plan that could release them all. In Theia's opinion, that was one of Mittens's problems: he wasn't willing to leave anyone behind. He wanted the best for everybody.

Theia did not have that problem. She was quite fine if she escaped alone. Preferred it, even, maybe. Nobody to worry about, or to take care of. She was so over other animals that she wasn't even sure she would go home if she got out. She might just live on her own, wild and free, embracing each day as a new adventure.

That would be the life, she thought. *That is who I am meant to be.*

"Little puppy livessss another day," Randy lamented. He was digesting and bored. "Too bad. I've alwayssss been curioussss what dog tassssstessss like."

"You're gross," a Golden Retriever named Apple said.

"Apple's an idiot, but he's right," Sal added. "If you don't have anything nice to say, shove it up your snake ass, Randy."

Theia kept licking her paw, ignoring the conversation happening around her. Nerd started to doze off behind the counter, as there would likely be no visitors for a few hours. Now that the animals were fed, many of them were ready for a nap, too.

Tired of resisting, Theia created a nest of her own in the back of her den, curled up inside, and drifted fast asleep.

CHAPTER III

This was her least favorite dream, because it wasn't fiction. It was a retelling of the events of how she ended up in the shelter.

Even though Theia was colorblind when her eyes were open, her dreams were a different story. She was allowed to color them in with her imagination. On this day, the sky was a magnificent orange. She woke up that morning next to her mother and father on a rug in their living room. Theia's people were dog breeders, and she had been a puppy from one of their litters. Before Theia existed, they had never held onto a puppy they had bred. They were all sold to presumably happy homes, and their lives were the transactional trade-in-stock of the breeders.

But once Theia was born, they made an exception. They had never met a dog like her before – which of course is true of every creature born – but there was just something special about her. So she received her forever name from them, and they kept her for themselves.

Theia was careful not to wake anybody up. She tiptoed to the kitchen and saw some kibble in a bowl. She ate it quickly, and then went outside using a small door within a door.

She sniffed at the air. Her nose told her she was up earlier than normal. The sun weighed down on her silver coat like a heated blanket, and tiny droplets of ivory foam fell from her rosy lips. She took a shit, scratched into the soil like a madwoman and then ran down the slope of the backyard to a corner of the tall green fence.

Theia had started to dig a hole there a few days earlier. The people hadn't seen it yet, so it was quite far along. She imagined she would probably have it wide enough to get through today, and then she would go see what was outside outside. She continued her excavation, feeling refreshed from her sleep and breakfast.

A shift in the wind later, the hole had been cleared enough for her to fit. Her head went through easily, and then she set her paws up front and pulled the rest of her body out like a cork. She tumbled feet over head, but she was free.

Her head ran in every direction and left her mind blank. She wasn't sure which way to go, but she knew she wanted to go. She figured she could come back and go a different way if it didn't work out, so she just started walking. She didn't know she was not going to have this chance again. In the real world, her body started to twitch.

Turn around! she screamed at herself. *Go back!*

Though she was a dog, she knew regret as well as anyone. Despite her knowing calls to herself, in the dream she kept trotting forward, queen of the neighborhood, goddess of the world. She came upon a blue cat, and this was the moment that changed her life.

Walk away! she pleaded. *This is when it happens!*

Not being able to change the course of the past, Theia confronted the cat.

"What's new, pussycat?" Theia asked, pleased in this greeting.

"Get away from me, dog," the cat warned. "This mouse is mine."

Theia looked under the cat. A tiny pink mouse was squirming under its paw, squealing for its life. Theia acted at once, without thought. She leaped into the cat, who lost its balance and fell backwards. The mouse seized the opportunity to escape and jumped under a nearby porch.

"You shouldn't have done that, dog," the cat scowled after pushing Theia aside.

Sleeping Theia's legs were starting to come alive. Her body was beginning to run, trying to help her escape from both the dream and the reality.

Theia growled at the cat. Its face grew wide in fear, and it turned around and ran away as fast as it could. Theia didn't have a moment to celebrate, however, as a man picked her up from behind and plunged a needle into her shoulder blade. The man was speaking to another man, but their voices were drowsy in her ears, like a vinyl record slowing down. As the world around Theia grew dark, the last thing she remembered seeing was a plate on the back of a van. She couldn't read it, obviously, but she recognized a picture on it. It was a picture of a fruit. Then she was out.

In real life, she was anything but. She was laying on her side, but in a full sprint now. Her blanket was pressed against the back of her cell, and she was making terrible scratching sounds against the metal floor below. The rest of the animals in the shelter were now awake, and shouting at her to wake her up, too.

She finally heard their calls and sat up, breathing heavily, embarrassed. Her entire body was hot, like the ashes after a fire dies out.

"Bad dreamssss?" Randy hissed.

CHAPTER IV

The other animals got back to minding their own business. Nerd was watching *Fantastic Planet*, a film that had fascinated Theia. She wasn't interested presently, however; she had to figure out a new plan.

Theia had been at the shelter for about a month now, if her nose was right. She hadn't learned much about the other animals because she didn't care for them and didn't see the point, as she had planned to escape the very first day. From what she overheard, though, some of them were like her; found and taken against their will. Some of them, however, had never seen or could remember anything but the animal shelter. It had been all they'd ever known. She pitied and envied them. They didn't know what they were missing, but also had nothing to miss.

She stood up to test out her paw, and it felt like a thorn was lodged in it. She could walk in circles in her quarters, but she limped as she did. Trying to make another break for it was out of the question for the time being; she was going to have to use her brain to stand a chance at getting out the door.

"Are you feeling anxious?" Mittens asked. The ferret was empathetic to a fault.

"I'm fine," Theia said, unsuccessfully conveying her bravado.

"I have bad dreams, too," he said. "I often have a dream where I'm floating. Up and up and up. And I'm reaching for anything to hold me down, and everything is out of my reach. As I float, it gets darker, and when I reach the blackest darkness, I can't breathe. That's usually when I wake up. It's hard to sleep for a long time after that."

Theia said nothing in return. She had been distracted by the movie, and it gave her an idea. If she could distract Nerd long enough, then maybe she could get through the door unnoticed, which would give her enough time to navigate the hallways to find a way outside.

She now conceded that in order to execute a plan, she would have to work with at least one of the other animals. Unfortunately for her, her best bet was the ferret.

""Hey, Mittens," Theia whispered, "Have you ever thought about getting out of here?"

"Not really, miss," Mittens said, with little conviction. "I don't mind it here."

Damn it, Theia thought. She looked around the room. The Pitbull, Sal, considered her a nuisance. Apple was an idiot. The snake was an asssshole. There were other dogs, plus cats and guinea pigs and a rabbit, but she didn't know their names.

"I would, however," Mittens added, "be willing to help you."

That was unexpected. Why would the ferret be willing to help someone with nothing in it for him? This made no sense to Theia. But she wasn't about to say no to some assistance. She was just going to have to be cautious.

"I was thinking that if someone could distract Nerd, then I would be able to get through the door," Theia said.

"How would I do that?" Mittens asked.

"I don't know," Theia admitted. "We would both have to get out of our cages. You would have to be the one to distract him. Long enough for him to not notice me."

"What if I was nice to him?" Mittens asked. This appeared to be his answer for everything. He thought that being nice would open all doors.

"Why would that help?" she asked.

"Because then he would trust me."

His answer seemed so simple, but he was right. If Nerd trusted Mittens, then maybe Nerd would take him out on his own accord. If Mittens could get out, then anything was possible.

"You have to do more than be nice," Theia said. "You have to be extraordinary."

"I could do a trick," Mittens thought aloud.

Theia started to ponder. What kind of stupid pet trick would get Nerd's attention, to the extent that he would have to pull him out of his crate?

"I'll think of something," Mittens said, and then added: "I think it's dinner time."

There were two feeding periods in the shelter: morning and evening. During both shifts, Nerd would have to fill out a report, confirming each animal was fed, and writing a description of their general well-being. Andrea was the person Nerd gave the reports to, so they regularly saw her twice a day. Visitors to the shelter did not come at scheduled times, nor particularly often. Sometimes, a visitor would take an animal out of their cage, and then a day or two later they would be returned. Sometimes, the animal never came back at all. Theia assumed that meant they had either found a new home, or had been put down. These observations weren't baseless; her many hours of watching science-fiction films had made her a very progressive thinker, as far as dogs go.

Nerd was finishing up a peanut butter and jelly sandwich as he walked over to the supply drawers. He proceeded to feed each animal in the same order he had that morning, making Theia last once again.

"I shouldn't even feed you . . . " Nerd said as stared into her cage. "You should have to earn your food by respecting me. The other pets do it."

He waved his arm behind him to display the animals he spoke of, and though they were generally not a fan of Theia and her disobedience, they universally disliked Nerd more. That was one of the things she couldn't reconcile; if they hated him as much as she did, why didn't they do anything about it?

"You take one step," Nerd threatened, "and I finish the job the door started on your leg."

He slowly opened her cage, but did so fully. You could see in his eyes that he wanted her to disobey. He wanted a reason. She sat on her tailless bottom, her eyes not shifting their lock on his. He grabbed a scoop of kibble, and made no care to place it directly in the bowl. Her dinner lined the wall of her cage. He pulled his hand out, and left the door open for a moment, testing her. She did not move. He shut the door.

After the animals had finished their food, Nerd dragged a big metal box full of gray sand into the middle of the room. This was the bathroom box. One by one, he leashed each and lead them into it. This was the one time a day they were allowed take a shit with any kind of normalcy, though they had to do so essentially on a stage while everyone else watched. The metal box had a pole extending vertically from one corner; Nerd would attach the leash to the pole while the animal did their business, checking and cleaning their cage in the meantime.

Once Theia was done, she was brought back into her crate, where she again kneaded her blanket into a nest. She licked her vagina aggressively, yawned, and then settled in to sleep for the night.

Nerd finished the evening report just before Andrea arrived to pick it up. She silently left it on the counter and walked over to Theia's bin. She crouched to be on her level. Theia looked to her.

"How are you doing, sweet girl?" she asked.

Theia averted her eyes and turned away.

"I understand," she said. "I'm sorry."

She stood up, walked back to the counter, picked up the report and didn't say another word as she left.

"Bitch," Nerd echoed, like he knew no better words to say.

He got up from his seat, turned off his computer and the monitor he used for movies, and did a quick last look at the animals. He turned off the light, blanketing them in darkness, and locked the door behind him.

Some of the dogs were snoring before he turned the key. Theia wasn't so lucky. She was terrified of falling back to sleep. She was unfortunate enough to be scared of both her dreams and her memories. She only wanted to run; she was strictly enforced to stay. Randy was peering at her through the dim, only adding ways she could feel horror. Her body was coiled like a notebook spiral.

A light tapping sound started trickling through the room. It sounded like the click of anticipatory claws. It persisted for hours, and Theia started to think that maybe she was imagining it, that her dreams were starting to creep out into reality. None of the other creatures had seemingly noticed or at least addressed the sound. Finally, it stopped.

"Miss?" a voice called through the darkness, comforting to her surprise.

"What is it, Mittens?" she asked.

"I've got it. I've got my trick."

CHAPTER V

Morning suddenly appeared. When Theia finally slept, it was because she was too tired to stay awake. Her exhaustion gave her the gift of dreamless rest. In any case, she was risen by the sound of the door opening, and Nerd starting his shift.

Her senses weren't immediately sharp, but she could tell he was late again. He stumbled through the motions again, beef stick in mouth, and started the feeding process. He looked half-asleep to Theia, maybe a victim of bad dreams, too. She could only hope.

He was standing in front of her den. This wasn't unusual, except now he had been there for longer than normal. She sniffed the air. Apprehensively, she took a step forward. Her paw still stung.

"Holy shit," Nerd said.

Theia took a step back, and then walked up to the door of her crate. She pressed her face against the door to try to see what was going on. Nerd was looking into Mittens's kennel, and he looked dumbfounded. Something astonishing was going on in there.

Nerd shut the cage with care, and then bent down and quickly opened Theia's.

"Don't you try anything," he warned again. He slapped a wave of kibble against the wall of her hut and slammed it shut. Behind him, Andrea walked in for the morning report and Nerd burst across the room towards her.

"You have to see this," Nerd insisted. He grabbed her wrist and pulled her back to Mittens's enclosure. Now they were both standing in front of Theia, and she still had no idea what was happening just inches above her.

"That . . . is incredible," Andrea said, which in itself sent a shock through Theia, as she had never heard Andrea agree with Nerd about anything.

"What do we do?" Nerd asked.

"Let me bring a few others here to see this," she said. She left immediately, and Nerd walked back behind the counter. He was humming a song as he turned on his computer and the big monitor. He put *Charlotte's Web* on the screen, which Theia had never seen but was too distracted to watch.

Soon, Andrea was back and she had brought more visitors with her. They came over and stood in a circle at the center of the shelter. Nerd came back to their wall and took Mittens out of his cage.

He did it, Theia thought. *I have to be ready.*

Nerd set Mittens down on the floor in the middle of all the people. He stood back and they all awaited Mittens's trick. Theia had to squeeze her head against the side of her coop, but she could see between their legs now.

For a moment, Mittens just stood there. His tiny left paw swept over his nose a few times, and the people did not appear to be impressed. Then he looked over at Theia, and gave her a little nod. Now was the time.

Theia had not noticed that sitting on the floor around Mittens were pieces of his food. Little kibbles, like she ate. He picked up a few, and then he did something she had never seen before. He began to juggle.

The people exploded with surprise. They were laughing and shoving one another, and Mittens kept juggling. Once he finished, they started to applaud, and talk amongst each other. Mittens noticed they weren't paying attention to him at all, and he darted over to Theia's kennel.

Mittens pushed the bolt to Theia's cell over, and the door swung wide open. He had done it. Theia was free. She burst out of her pen and headed straight for the door, which had been left ajar by the visitors. By this time, Nerd had noticed the ferret was gone; by the time his eyes had located Mittens, Theia was halfway across the shelter.

"No!" he hollered, and dove in-between two of the others. He grabbed one of Theia's back legs. Normally, she would have been able to push herself out of his grasp; he was barely hanging on. As it was, she put pressure on her front paws, and her left gave out. She collapsed.

In all this excitement, Mittens made the realization that yet again no eyes were on him. If he were put back in his cage now, there wouldn't be another chance like this. They would most certainly be more careful and most definitely think twice before taking an animal out.

With this thought, Mittens himself ran towards the front of the shelter. He slinkied his way as swiftly as he could and reached the door, which was open just a crack, before anybody noticed. He took a quick look back, and he met Theia's eyes. He couldn't imagine what she was thinking. He had no time to stop and figure it out or explain. He escaped over the threshold.

As the others helped Nerd secure Theia and put her back in her cell, Andrea made the realization first.

"Where's the ferret?" she asked. As soon as the question was posed, the people were scattered and sent both directions down the hallway outside the door, which shut behind them.

Theia stared out at her fleeing chance, by now far gone, and let herself feel a familiar resentment for the weasel who got away.

CHAPTER VI

The search for Mittens went into the night.

People came in and out of the shelter, looking for updates and offering tips. He seemed to have disappeared as soon as he slipped between the crack. They marveled at the little rodent's ability as a magician.

An escape artist for sure, Theia thought, *and definitely not a friend.*

The other animals could sense her new level of discontent. Her vibe previously radiated at a simmer, but presently boiled over the bars of her cage. The difference now was no one dare speak up to her, not even to break the tension. The shelter was quieter among the animals than it had been since Theia's arrival.

Nerd almost forgot dinner, and likely would have if Randy hadn't spit a pointed hiss in his direction. He hastily delivered their food, barely turned around to do one last check and then shut down his equipment. He slapped the lights off and locked the door behind him.

The animals started to get into their sleeping positions. Theia, desperate to keep the attention on if the lights weren't, licked herself with sloppy abandon, like a person deliberately chewing with their mouth open. No one bit, and the room stayed silent.

Despite being severely upset with Mittens, she realized that his absence meant that no one would be checking in with her tonight. The pain of not having even an acquaintance in the world felt worse than her anger. This surprised her, and it made her even more anxious to get out.

Hours passed, and Theia couldn't sleep. Between the dreams and her dashed hopes, her mind wouldn't slow down enough for her to latch onto sheep. She wondered about her mom and dad. Were they worried about her? Were they disappointed? Did they ever try to find her, to make sure she was okay?

Those questions made her uncomfortable. Most questions did. She felt like most other animals must not ask themselves as many. She looked around the room; they were all sound asleep, not a problem to any of their names.

Lucky, she thought. *Everyone is lucky but me.*

Her wallowing brought a heaviness to her eyelids, which sent her to sleep.

What felt like seconds later, the light struck on and she was wide awake, her muscles aching from a restless sleep and an unanchored mind. Nerd dragged his way across the floor like a slug, an apple in his hand. Andrea came in right behind him, and they appeared to not have any news of Mittens. Apparently, Nerd had been looking for him all night, and came up with nothing. Andrea offered to do the morning feeding and report for Nerd, and he was more than happy to oblige.

Andrea came around the pens, and it was like a ray of light from a cloud. All the animals were very receptive to her, even Randy; she had a level of respect for each one, and treated them with kindness. Nerd looked a combination of annoyed and jealous from behind the counter; this morning he was playing a film called *Dr. Doolittle*, another movie for children that Theia didn't especially care for.

She despised nearly aspect of Nerd, but she did love science-fiction, which was his favorite genre, as well. So on the days when she couldn't escape, she could escape, if only for a few hours. Animals don't strictly understand the English language, but they understand tone quite well; often, tone told them more than words ever could. Even when Theia couldn't comprehend the science behind the art, she understood the emotion and the action, the amazing fantasy of it all. She was a dog with an imagination, which made her the most dangerous kind of all.

When Andrea finally came to Theia's lodge, it didn't seem like she was being punished; it felt like she was being saved for last. Andrea carefully put her kibble in the dish, and scratched Theia behind the ears.

Oh, that's good, Theia thought.

She stretched out, her paws creating gaps in-between. She shook the stress off from head to tail, her gold collar shimmering like a tambourine. Then, she subtly turned her body ninety degrees and looked at Andrea with an unmistakable smile.

"Would you like me to scratch your bottom, Theia?" she asked.

Her tongue rolled out of her mouth to confirm. Andrea's fingernails dug deep into Theia's hindquarters, imitating the movement of sandpaper. This was the first time Theia had felt good since being brought to the shelter. She never wanted it to end.

Of course, it did, like everything does. Andrea rubbed the top of Theia's nose, right between her eyes.

"You're such a sweet girl," she said as she shut the kennel, and then put the feeding supplies away.

The mood in the room had dramatically shifted during this feeding service. Unfortunately, it did not make Theia want to stay. If anything, it reminded her how alienated she was from the rest of these animals, and how much she missed the outside world. Her resolve was restored; runaway weasel or not, she would devise a new plan to get out.

The dinner service came and passed and still no Mittens. Chatter among the shelter was genial; they were all quite impressed with lunch still, and they had seemed to find a feeling that hadn't been there before: hope. Theia stayed out of the conversation, for she would not be infected by these delusional creatures. She again pitied them, but their intent to stay further convinced her that escape for herself was possible.

After lights out, the animals were soon slumbering. Theia was aimlessly plotting, having trouble finding a strong thought that stuck. Mittens may have been naive and cloying, but he was also helpful and clearly not afraid to take action. Maybe her problem was in planning; maybe if she just let the story play out, she would be able to react

when the plan revealed itself. She would just have to be
ready.

She slept with one eye subconsciously open.

CHAPTER VII

Mittens was a Christmas gift. An albino ferret, he was white and rare as snow in the southeast. He was purchased at a pet store in a mall, one of the last of its kind. On Christmas Eve, he was received by four children, not one of them over the age of six.

His early life was torture. The children had never had a pet before, and their parents had little to do with them. Both worked full-time jobs, leaving them in the care of a single nanny, who could barely keep their schedule, much less have her eyes on them with any manner of consistency.

They would hurt Mittens. They would chase him until he couldn't run anymore. They would pull him – one child on his arms, another on his legs – stretching him as far apart as they could, until he squealed. He was stepped on, spit on, shouted towards, screamed at. One of the children put his head in their mouth.

An animal's faith is hard to describe. But each kind is different, if some not so different than others. Mittens believed in a kind of karma, which many ferrets believe in. They believe that the skills you possess during your life transfer into the afterlife. It's one of the reasons ferrets are so cunning and quick to disappear; they believe they can use these abilities to fool Death herself once she comes.

And it's the reason that Mittens always chose to be kind, even in the face of terrible abuse. He believed that if he could be skillful with kindness, he would bring that gift with him to the afterlife, and be able to teach it to any ferret who had passed without learning or receiving it during their lifetimes.

This ability to be kind almost killed him on countless occasions, and he never regretted it once.

The scariest time happened to be the last. The oldest boy, an unholy combination of strength and stubbornness, had been particularly challenging on this day. He was chasing Mittens with a squirt gun filled with his own urine, and every time Mittens would disappear, the child would cry and beg for him to return. Mittens would come when called, without hesitation, to make sure he was okay. Sure enough, the kid was full of shit and would start shooting piss at him again.

The final time Mittens came out to check on the child, he picked Mittens up.

"You're dirty and wet," the boy said. "You need to be dried off."

The boy then brought Mittens to the drying machine, where he was put inside and turned on permanent press. Twenty minutes later, the nanny heard his squeaks and found him in the machine. She reported what had happened to the parents, and they decided immediately, for the sake of the animal, to bring Mittens back to the store.

Unfortunately, the store (and the mall) had permanently closed. So, instead, they took Mittens to a nearby animal shelter, where they happily accepted him (and the fee for his deposit). His time at this shelter was short-lived, however; after a few hours of sitting in a hot cage in a dust-filled room, a man in a white coat arrived to move him. He stuck a needle above Mittens's shoulder blade, and Mittens blacked out. He had no idea how long he was sleeping, but he vividly remembers his disjointed dreams, and when he woke up he was in the cage at the animal shelter where he later met Theia.

He was thankful for Theia. She allowed him to put his beliefs back into practice. In his dreams, he denounced kindness; all it had brought him was an enormous amount of pain. He turned away the spirits in the darkness who needed his help, because he didn't think he could take another moment of despair.

Theia woke up his heart. She reminded him that caring about others is why he was still here; her selfishness was a reflection of who he could have been, and he was allowed to denounce that version of himself. He didn't know what his service was going to bring him. He didn't know it was going to literally set him free.

When he escaped from the shelter, he ended up in a hallway. His only options were left or right; he was facing a wall on the other side of the door. The right side almost immediately split into two more directions; the left went on a long ways, and he figured it would give him plenty of time to see somebody who was coming. He ran down that side for a few moments, and it was pretty plain. The walls and doors were all the same light gray color and barely distinguished with marks. There was no telling them apart, as far as Mittens was concerned. A sound from behind him was the door reopening from the shelter; at that exact moment, Mittens noticed a small vent on the wall to his left. He easily lifted up the plastic grate and slipped inside.

The vent went in all directions. It was comfortably warm, so Mittens figured it was a heating vent. He could have found a worse hiding spot, he was certain of that. With no other options, he started exploring the system. When it became too warm, he reasoned he was getting close to whatever was making the heat and turned around.

At certain points, the vent system went vertically, and he was able to climb up it. Now he had the ability to be over rooms and see inside them. He couldn't make sense of what most of the rooms contained. But he kept moving, and when he didn't have any energy, he slept. After a few cycles of this, he wasn't sure how long he had been gone.

He eventually lost all sense of direction. He had decided that he had to get back to the shelter, but he wanted to get there from inside. He scurried to an area he hadn't been to yet, and the vent grew terribly cold. He kept on and found himself over a massive, cavernous room. The problem with this room was not that he didn't understand what was in it; it was that he understood it all too clearly. He thought to himself:

How will I be kind to Theia when I break her heart?

CHAPTER VIII

Theia woke up slowly, another restless night. She sniffed the air and could smell it was morning, but the room was still dark. The other animals were still asleep, making assorted sounds in slumbering concert. The other animals, with the exception of Sal.

"How you feeling today, princess?" Sal asked, between licks of her coffee-colored coat.

"Leave me alone, Sal," Theia said.

"You have a real attitude problem, you know that?" Sal said. "This place isn't all that bad. It's your attitude that smells like my business."

"You don't know anything about me," Theia spit back. "I don't know anything about you and, honestly, I don't care. I don't belong here. I belong out there."

"What's out there that you want so bad?" Sal asked.

"Possibilities," Theia said. Her vague answer was something she had never questioned before. The Pitbull was making her second-guess herself.

"That's a stupid answer," Sal said. "Selfish, too."

Theia growled at Sal. Sal stood up and growled back. The other animals started to wake up to the commotion, and the front door opened. Nerd backed into the room, box in hand, and set it on the counter. He turned on the light and the rumbling dogs quieted down, their eyes still fixed each other.

Oblivious, Nerd went about his daily routine. He turned on his computer, put *Short Circuit* on the monitor and started feeding the inmates. He was still full of his miserable disdain, but his heart didn't appear to be in it today. Andrea walked in as he finished the morning report.

"Still no ferret?" he asked.

"No, still missing," she replied. "Look, we don't like one another. That's fine, except I feel like I would be a much better fit running the shelter."

"The director of the shelter thinks otherwise," he said.

"The director of the shelter is your father," she pointed out, adding, "I think he could be convinced otherwise."

"Get out," he said.

Without another word, she took the report off the counter and left. Nerd slowly got up and put his hands on the counter, then turned around sharply and threw his chair against the wall. He grunted, which the animals understood perfectly. He walked across the room, picked up his chair and set it back in its place. He slouched down in it, and mindlessly stared at his monitor.

A few hours later, Andrea returned, but this time with another man. The man was well-dressed and wore a formal hat. Nerd immediately stood up at attention.

"Father," Nerd greeted him, looking nervously over at Andrea. "What brings you here?"

"I'm just doing a regular screening of the animal shelter," his father, Neil, answered. "Andrea tells me there is room for improvement, so I wanted to see the state of things as they were."

Neil walked over to the cages, Nerd and Andrea close behind.

"Quite sad, aren't they?" Neil noticed.

"One of my ideas is that we could let the animals interact with one another," Andrea said. "Especially the dogs. It's quite inhumane to keep them to themselves, all day, every day."

She went over to Theia's crate and opened the door. Theia did not know how to react. Was this the moment she had been waiting for? Before she could answer her own thought, a leash was attached to her collar. She slowly stepped out of her box, and was led over to another cage; inside this den was Sal.

Andrea opened Sal's crate, and Sal retreated to the back. She held the leash firmly as Theia was gently led inside. Theia, unsure of how to proceed, wrinkled her nose and let out an uncertain whine.

"Follow my lead," Sal said, as she pushed her front side downward and displayed her bottom. Theia walked over and smelled her butt.

"Okay, Theia," Sal said, her teeth gritted but grinning. "It's your turn."

Theia's eyes rolled. She obediently turned her body around and let Sal do the same. They both looked at the woman for approval.

"See?" Andrea said. "They're just craving interaction. I'm going to leave them together for a little while."

Andrea shut the door and latched it. She, Neil and Nerd walked back to the counter and continued their conversation, leaving Theia and Sal stuck together.

"Look, you said you don't care about me," Sal started. "But it's like you said: you don't know anything about me. What if I told you how I got here?"

"It's not like I'm going anywhere," Theia said, trying to find a place to get comfortable.

"That's the spirit," Sal said.

Then she told Theia her story:

"When I was a puppy, I thought I was the most-loved dog in the world. I was in a litter of just two, and my sister passed away when we were really little, before I could even really remember her. Her name was Jacqueline. My mom told me that before I was taken away.

"I guess the people who owned my mom never wanted any puppies, so they were trying to sell me as soon as I could see. I met so many humans, and they adored me. They loved my puppy cheeks, my fur, my huge paws. But none of them wanted to take me home.

"I don't know if you know what they say about Pitbulls. 'Mean dogs,' they say, like they could ever know what's in our hearts. So, while everyone I met as a puppy loved me, no one could take me home knowing what I would grow up to be.

"When I got a little older, the people said they had no other choice but to get rid of me. So I went to something called a foster home. It was nice, and the new people weren't mean to me, but they were cold and they kept me at a distance. Not like when I was a puppy. And just as I was getting settled in, I was moved again. To another foster home, like the last one. And this happened again and again and again."

Sal's eyes were wet. Theia extended her paw and laid it on Sal's.

"At least here they don't pretend. They don't pretend to love me or care about me. They treat me like the world sees me: a bad dog. And that's why I don't care to leave. I get fed, I have a bed. And they don't bullshit me about how they feel."

"Don't you feel like you deserve more?" Theia asked.

"Sometimes," Sal said. "Sometimes I don't."

Theia, feeling sympathy for Sal and missing something from home, got up from her spot and snuggled into Sal. Sal rested her head on top of Theia's. During the story, neither dog had noticed that Andrea and Neil had left. Nerd had now walked over the cage and was opening it.

"Playdate's over," Nerd said, reaching into the lodge with a leash. Both dogs huddled closer together. "Come on now."

Nerd shoved his entire hand under Sal's gold collar, grabbing it in a fist. Theia was pushed aside, and she growled.

"You want some, bitch?" Nerd asked Theia.

"It's not worth it," Sal said, and she had barely said it before Theia latched onto Nerd's wrist with her teeth.

He let out a guttural scream, and then squeezed Theia by a tuft of hair behind her head. He shook her violently, and then threw her across the room, into the cages on the other side.

The other animals were indignant. They were barking and meowing and screeching in opposition. Theia wasn't moving, and Sal was in shock. Nerd let her go and shut the door behind him, and went over to the unconscious Theia. He picked her up, unconcerned with her well-being, and laid her back in her cage.

Barely breathing, Theia was finally able to sleep.

CHAPTER IX

"Theia," she could hear through the darkness. "Theia, are you okay?"

Her eyes slowly opened. Her body had never felt this kind of pain before. She was coated in it. As her vision adjusted, she realized that it was night. The lights were off, but she could sense the animals were still awake.

"I'm . . . fine," Theia answered. Sal had been the one who was calling to her. Theia looked around her crate. Feeding time had obviously passed, and no kibble had been placed in her dish. She wasn't brought out, either.

"You shouldn't have done that," Sal said. "Is anything broken?"

"No . . . I don't think so," Theia said.

"That man is the baddest," Apple said. Apple was an honest, simple dog, so he did mean the worst man, not the coolest. "I will bite him for you if you want me to."

"No, Apple, don't do that," Theia said. "Be a good dog."

"Okay," Apple said. "I like being a good dog."

"What's the plan, Theia?" Sal asked. Her question confused Theia.

"I don't understand," Theia said.

"To get you out of here," she replied.

Theia didn't have a plan. She had tried to think of one on her own, and couldn't. She had decided to wait for an opportunity to present itself, and when it did, she didn't act. On top of all of that, she had just made the worst possible decision by biting Nerd.

"I don't know, Sal," Theia said. "I think I may have just made a huge mistake."

"No," Sal said. "You didn't. Never apologize for when you have to bite. When you live in a world that hurts you and doesn't listen, sometimes all you have left is to hurt them back. But it's not who you are. It's who they made you be."

"I'm not so sure," Theia said.

"Well, I am," Sal assured her. "Get your rest. We'll try to figure something out in the morning."

Sal turned in. The other animals had already begun to rest. Theia wasn't sure it was going to be so easy for her, but her body disagreed. It needed to heal, and it slowed down her thoughts so she could breathe. She took a shit in the corner of her cage, as far away from where she slept as she could (which was still not far enough), and fell soundly asleep.

As her body twitched gently through the night, a nightmare filled her mind. In the dream, she was free-falling through outer space with no end in sight. Just a perpetual state of downward motion through a star-lit abyss. Time is abstract in sleep, so after an infinite flight, she was slammed into an asteroid made of twisted metal bars. The asteroid was alive, and the bars twitched out like mangled spider legs; they wrapped around her, and she was trapped inside. She peered through the asteroid cage, and saw a mysterious world ahead. It grew closer and closer. She entered its atmosphere, and the planet didn't look like she expected it to look. She braced for impact, but right before hitting the ground –

She woke up.

She must have felt Nerd coming, because just a moment later he opened the door. When the light came on, Theia could clearly see he was looking in her cage. His face held a mixture of anxiety and relief. In his mind, Nerd resolved that she was alive and didn't have words to use against him, so he was in the clear. Theia very much felt a different way.

Nerd fed Theia first, which was more an admission of his guilt than anything else. When he opened the door to her cage, she did not flinch. She did not move. She stood her ground, and stared him in the eyes. She did not blink.

He gave her an extra portion of food, which was not extra at all, but what she should have received the night before. She was not grateful, because all she got was what she deserved either way. In the bottom of her throat, barely audible, she revved like an engine. Nerd placed his hand on his other wrist, which had been bandaged and concealed under a long-sleeve shirt. Theia noted that maybe he didn't want anyone to know that she bit him, either.

The morning report was done well before Andrea arrived. She looked skeptical. She took a walk around the pens to do her own wellness check. When she got to Theia's crate, she stopped. Theia looked right into her eyes and she knew. The way one knows when another is in pain. She turned away and addressed Nerd.

"I appreciate you dropping off the evening report last night," she said. "Your father and I talked at length about the future of the shelter. I told him about my intentions and requested an assessment of both our skills.

Next week, he's coming back to see how we are with the animals and who he feels is better qualified to run it."

"That's bullshit," he said.

"It's not," she said. "Be ready. I want the best person for this job to have it, and if you want to make it easy for me that's your decision."

She picked up the report and was out the door before Nerd could say another word. The animals couldn't understand many of the words, but some could relatively understand the situation. There was a potential opportunity for the nice woman to take the bad man's place. That would be good.

Nerd strained his voice making more unintelligible noises. He went to throw his chair again but stopped himself with the chair in his hands above his head. He set it down, his teeth flat together. He sat.

There he sat for the rest of the day. An atrocious smell started to fill the room during the late afternoon, and Nerd put a prop between the door and frame to let some fresh air from the outside in. He hadn't realized the smell was coming from Theia's cage.

Dinner came, and he returned to the normal feeding schedule, Theia being last. After they ate, he took her out to use the bathroom box he had dragged out. He latched her leash onto the metal pole on the corner of the box, and went over to check her cage.

"Are you kidding me?!" Nerd screamed, his shrill voice filling the shelter. He discovered Theia's shit in the corner of her crate, and he was consumed with rage. She couldn't control her reaction; her body went limp and she tucked her head in, waiting for him to come over and hurt her.

She listened as he stomped towards her. Suddenly, something dropped right next to Theia. It was breathing heavily and she felt a tug on her collar. She looked up, and standing beside her was Mittens. He had dropped onto the box from a vent above, and unhooked her collar from the leash.

"I'm sorry," Mittens said, out of breath.

"Why are you sorry?" Theia asked.

"Because what is out there is not what you think is out there," Mittens said.

"What do you mean?" she asked.

"You have to go see for yourself," he said. "Now go!"

Nerd was shocked to see the ferret fall from the sky. Now Theia was unleashed, and the door was cracked open. This was her shot.

She burst out of the box and headed for the door. She approached the opening. Like Mittens before her, she turned around and looked at the shelter once more.

And then Theia escaped.

CHAPTER X

Theia wasted no time. She went right, towards the immediate split, and then took another right. There were no people to be seen. She kept running as fast as she could, and she hadn't run like this since the day she was taken. It felt good.

This hall was long and there were doors that all looked the same. She was looking for a window. A window would show her the outside and she would be able to figure it out from there. She took off to the end of the hall, and it split again. Not taking her time to consider it, she immediately turned left. She took a few more steps when a man in a white coat peered out of an open doorway.

"What's that now?" the man said, clearly stupefied. He disappeared into the room he stood from, and then two more people came out with him, charging down the hall to Theia.

She immediately turned her stubby tail and darted the opposite way. The trio of humans in lab coats took flight behind her. She kept running, passing the initial hallway she came from. Moments later, another hall appeared on her left. She didn't hesitate in taking it.

Immediately, there was a woman standing above her. She screamed, and Theia heeled back, letting out a yip. She ran under the woman's legs and kept going. The first three people came barreling around the corner and knocked the woman down, falling head over themselves.

Straight ahead, there were double doors propped open. With nowhere else to go, she committed forward. The hall got colder as she approached, and she leaped inside a large, cavernous room.

At this sight, she finally took a pause. Breathing heavily, she stared at the giant window installed at the far end of the room. She recognized what she was looking at. It was a night sky, full of stars. But there was something hanging overhead, just out of sight.

She walked slowly towards the curved glass, and it came into view. Theia was an imaginative dog, but she couldn't have made this up. As the object came into view, she fully understood what she was looking at: it was the Earth.

How is this possible? she thought to herself.

From the films she had seen, there was the Earth, where she lived, and there was another place you could see at night: the Moon. Making this leap in logic would be difficult for a human, but for a dog it was nearly impossible to understand.

Theia understood it all the same. She was on the Moon, and the life she longed for was far, far away.

As all of this sunk in, the humans had now caught up to her. The man who first saw her picked her up and checked her collar.

"Theia?" he smiled. "That's too funny."

She was brought to a room that was not the shelter and placed on a cold metal table. They checked her vitals and made a full diagnostic report on her condition. She overheard words like "sprained" and "broken" and their tone confirmed what she already knew.

They wrapped up her left paw, tight as a noose. There were a few humans taking turns looking at her, coming in and out of the room. She was slowly coming down from everything that had happened, with no bottom in sight. Her anxiety amplified her breathing.

When they were satisfied with their results, the man from earlier came to take her to the shelter. He carried her all the way back, through the unremarkable halls that Theia had run so brilliantly through. He scratched her behind the ears, which wasn't entirely unwelcome. When they arrived, Nerd had already left for the day. This was also not unwelcome.

The man walked through the dark shelter and put Theia back into her crate. She had been fed and allowed to go to the bathroom in the other room, so she was ready to close her eyes and try to forget this day.

The man left and locked the door behind him. Theia could tell that none of the other animals were sleeping, but she knew if she said nothing first, none of them would bother her.

So she said nothing first.

CHAPTER XI

"Good morning, miss," Mittens said from up above.

"Good morning, Mittens," Theia replied. "I don't feel like talking today."

"I understand," he said. "Though . . . I will tell you that sometimes talking about it will help you feel better."

"Nothing," she said, "will make me feel better about what I know now."

Getting outside was the only thing that had kept Theia going. She hadn't cared how selfish she was being, because she knew that she wasn't going to be around for long anyway. Now the reality of how awful she had been to the other animals was sticking to her insides. She wanted to simply say sorry, and couldn't motivate her heart to move.

The morning feeding came and passed. Theia could barely eat. The shelter hummed like nothing had changed, and Theia had to remind herself that for them nothing had.

She (and Mittens, she remembered) had this information all to themselves.

Or did they? Now she wondered how many of the other animals knew where they were. The idea that any or all of them could and didn't tell her was infuriating. They probably mocked her when she was gone, reenacting how they supposed she reacted to the revelation.

"Who knew?" she blurted out.

The others looked at her with genuine curiosity. None of them seemed to know what she was accusing them of.

"Who knew what, Theia?" Sal asked.

"Who else knew that this shelter was on the Moon?" Theia asked again. The shelter went completely quiet.

And then erupted into laughter.

"Sssstupid dog!" Randy hissed. "Who ssssspiked Theia'ssss water dissssh?"

"Theia," Mittens whispered. "The other animals do not know. The other animals could not understand."

This broke Theia's heart more. Now she realized that she would have to live with this feeling alone. The feeling of knowing there was nowhere to run to. The certainty that her future was decided and over.

The shelter quieted down and soon enough dinner was served. Nerd put the new food on top of the old food Theia couldn't bring herself to eat. He wouldn't even look at her. That suited her fine. She ignored her food once more.

When *Jurassic Park* on the monitor ended, Nerd turned it and his computer off. Andrea walked in to pick up both daily reports and saw that Theia had returned.

"Sweet girl," she said and smiled. Without hesitation, she walked over and opened up Theia's cage.

"She just ran away!" Nerd yelled.

"I completely understand why!" she shouted back.

Andrea pressed her thumbs into Theia's cheeks, pushing her lips up into a smile. She gave her a few more bottom scratches and then closed the door again. She picked up the reports and said nothing else to Nerd before leaving. Nerd picked up his things and did the same, turning off the lights.

The shelter quieted down and started their sleep. Theia rapidly dug into her blanket to freshen it, and then curled as close as she could to the back of her kennel.

"Theia?" a voice called from the darkness.

She ignored it.

"Theia," Apple said again.

"What is it, Apple?" Theia asked.

"I just wanted to say, I know what it's like to be sad." Apple was looking at her through his bars. He was a stupid creature, but he was beautiful. Luxurious golden fur wrapped his plush face and body.

"I'm not sad," Theia said.

"You are sad," Apple reiterated. "I know what sad is, and you are sad."

"How do you know what sad is, Apple?" Theia asked.

And then Apple told her his story.

CHAPTER XII

Apple was the luckiest dog.

His owner was a man named Will. Will was the nicest man. When Apple was a puppy, he was left in a box next to a gravel road. Will, who lived up the road, was on his morning run when he found him. The box said FREE on the side. Will thought he was the luckiest man, and he was right.

He brought Apple home and named him that because it was his favorite fruit, and this dog that he had found was his favorite dog. He took Apple to the store with him and bought two red bowls, a bag of dog food and a collar. On his collar, he put a tag shaped like an apple that read Apple, so nobody would forget.

Will lived on a small farm. This gave Apple plenty of room to run, so he did. He ran in the morning, and in the afternoon, and then he took a nap, and then ran again in the evening. Sometimes, Will would run with him. Sometimes he would throw something for Apple to bring back. Apple would sometimes not bring it back, because Apple fancied himself a bit of a comedian.

Will was often happy. When he was happy, Apple would do anything he could to make him happier. Will was sometimes sad. When he was sad, Apple would do everything he could to make him better. Will felt feelings that Apple didn't understand, and when that happened, Apple would just be there.

One day, Apple and Will went for a run. It was a normal day, and it was nice. Will was having problems keeping up, and Apple was nudging him along playfully. Will tripped on the gravel road, and he started to bleed. He wrapped himself up, but when they got home, the bleeding would not stop. Will looked worried, and Apple did not understand, so he made sure to just be there.

Will was gone for a whole day. The neighbor came over to check on Apple and let him outside. Apple was now feeling a new feeling, and he did not like it.

After another day, Will came back. Now Apple was happy and he knew this feeling and it was good. But Will was sad. He held Apple's face, and his eyes were wet.

Apple didn't know what to do, so he made sure to just be there. He licked Will's face to show him he was there.

Will didn't run very much anymore. Apple missed running with Will, but Will was home and that was more important than running. He would leave sometimes, but he always came back. Will always came back, because he loved Apple, the luckiest dog in the world.

One time Will came back with a bed that they put in the big room next to the front door. Will spent a lot of time in the bed, and now other people were stopping by often. Apple loved other people, but they were taking time away from Will, and this made him feel sad.

He could tell this made Will sad, too, because now Will was sad all the time. He never ran. He laid in the bed and his eyes were wet a lot. Apple was very confused by all of this, but the one thing he knew he could do was be there.

On the last day, Will said a lot of words to Apple. Apple was never a smart dog, but he understood this. Will said:

"I was the luckiest man."

And even though Will never understood him when he spoke, Apple said:

"I am the luckiest dog."

And then Will was gone. People came and took him away, and they didn't know what to do with Apple. The people said they had a problem looking at Apple, because he just reminded them all of Will.

Eventually, he was dropped off at a dark place he did not like the smell of.

A sharp needle in his back made him tired.

And when he woke up, he was here.

And every day, at least once, Apple feels sad.

CHAPTER XIII

Theia's eyes were wet now, too. The animals had all woken up and tuned in to Apple's story. Theia could see their eyes reflecting the little light in the shelter. His story had touched them all.

"Mittens," Theia called up.

"What is it?" Mittens said in-between sniffles.

"You opened my cage before to set me free," she said. "Could you come down and do it again?"

"I suppose I could," he said. There were rattling sounds above, and after a moment, Mittens was on the ground. He unlocked the door to Theia's pen, and she butted her head against it to step outside.

"Are you trying to break out again?" Sal asked. "Nerd will kill you!"

"Yessss, puppy, yessss!" Randy encouraged.

"No," Theia said. "I want to go over to Apple."

Theia and Mittens walked across the floor to Apple's crate, and Mittens opened it. Apple sniffed the air and was apprehensive. He slowly walked out to meet them. Theia started to go around him.

"What are you doing?" he asked.

"I was going to sniff your butt," she said.

"That's nasty business," he told her.

She stopped and came back to his front. She started licking his cheek, cleaning up the wet that had fallen from his eyes. All the animals were watching intently from their boxes, not entirely sure what to make of the moment. Theia realized that this was her chance to make amends.

"I'm sorry," she started. "To you, Apple, and to all of you. I have not been a good dog. I've treated you poorly, and spent all of my time here thinking about myself. I'm an asshole!"

The shelter laughed when she said this. She smiled, too, and she meant it. She had been an asshole. She couldn't even explain why. For some reason, the idea of running wherever she wanted to was more important than the real world that was happening around her. That wasn't fair, and instead of just barking about it, she had to do something.

"We're going to make this shelter a better place," she continued. "I don't know how, but I know we'll figure it out. Together."

She rubbed her face against Apple's, gave Mittens a kiss, and then walked back to her crate. Apple returned to his, and Mittens shut both doors. He climbed back up to his pen and locked himself back in.

After an hour, most of the animals had gone back to sleep. Theia was feeling a little better, but still restless. A voice from above had one last thing to add.

"Theia," Mittens said. "I know none of us know how to make this place better, but I've noticed that Nerd and Andrea have been upset with each other lately. What if there were a way to get rid of Nerd? Then maybe Andrea would take care of us. That would be better, right?"

"It would," Theia agreed. It wasn't a plan, but it was something to think about. And so she did, until her eyes closed nearly all the way, a sliver of white still glowing as she started to dream.

She was in a massive field of short grass with no end or people in sight. So she did what she longed to do and ran. She ran and ran and when she looked down, she saw that the grass wasn't moving. She was getting nowhere, no matter how fast she pumped her legs.

She stood still, and the grass fell from beneath her. She was suddenly plunged into absolute blackness. She stared at the dark around her, and in the corner of her eye she watched a star come to life. One by one, more stars joined it, and soon she was adrift in a fully realized sky.

She immediately felt scared. Space went on forever, and there was nothing to tether her or propel her in any direction. Her limbs frantically swam about and she barely spun around. She did not like this version of freedom.

"Theia," she heard a voice call from somewhere.

She spun back around and there was Mittens. Behind him was Sal, Apple and the rest of the animals in the shelter. They threw out a rope for her to grab.

"Take it!" they told her.

She was about to put her paws around it, when she looked down and saw that it wasn't a rope at all. It was a snake. It was Randy. He bared his fangs, and just as his head raised –

She woke up.

It was morning, and she took a look around the shelter. She peered up at Randy, and he was already staring at her. His tongue flipped out and he smiled as he asked:

"Bad dreamssss, puppy?"

CHAPTER XIV

She shook off the dream as breakfast was served. She had caught up to the old kibble in the bowl she was avoiding and was looking forward to fresh food. Nerd walked in and was clearly distraught. He rushed through feeding without turning on his computer or monitor, and the air was tense.

"What's his problem, you think?" Sal asked.

"Poop in his butt hair," Apple said with absolute seriousness.

"Maybe," Theia said. "Maybe it has to do with Andrea."

Like her number was called, Andrea appeared through the door. Nerd was intentionally taking his time on the report. He made no haste to finish though she was there to pick it up.

"You're three minutes early," he said.

"Why are you like this?" she asked. "Is it because Wednesday is only two days away and you're worried this might be the last forty-eight hours you spend behind that counter?"

Nerd glared at her. She stared at him, stoic, until he gulped.

"Here," he said, handing her the report. She smiled as wide as her face allowed, and was gone. Theia was trying to decode their conversation.

"I think something is happening soon," Theia said. "A battle."

The animals were skeptical. They had not seen any human battle in the shelter, and they could see no reason why they would start now.

"Mittens, you were talking about getting rid of Nerd, right?" Theia asked. "How would we even do that?"

"I know how . . ." an ominous voice echoed from the highest cage in the corner. It was like gravel shaking in a tin can, this voice that Theia had never heard before.

"Who's that?" she asked.

"It is me, Murdery," the voice answered. Out of the shadows in the box emerged a hairless cat with enormous eyes. Theia had not seen nor heard this cat the entire time she had been at the shelter.

"They brought her in when you escaped," Mittens told her, his voice shaking.

"How do we get rid of Nerd?" she asked.

"That is easy . . . " she said. "We murder him."

"Okay, bitch is insane," Sal said.

"What do you know about murder, Murdery?" Theia asked.

"When I was but a small kit . . . " Murdery started. "I was different from my brothers and sisters. They would frolic in the fields, singing songs of high hopes and wild dreams. When I was six months old, I murdered a nest of baby robins."

"Do you mean you ate the eggs?" Mittens asked.

"IT WAS MURDER," Murdery confirmed. She continued:

"Then, when I was a year old, I murdered all of my brothers and sisters. Their bodies had disappeared without a trace, and I was the culprit."

"You actually killed them?" Theia asked. "They didn't just run along somewhere else?"

"IT WAS MURDER," Murdery asserted. Some of the animals were very frightened by this story so far. Murdery had a very imposing presence.

"But I saved the most murder for last," she said.

"What does that even mean?" Sal asked.

"One day, I murdered all of the humans in my house. They were all gone. I murdered the man and the woman and the children and the mice and the couch – "

"Did you just say you murdered the couch?" Theia asked.

"Those people definitely just moved out of the house," Sal said.

"IT WAS MURDER," Murdery insisted.

"Okay, we're done talking now," Theia tried to say politely. "Nice to meet you, Murdery."

"Murder . . . " she could be heard whispering as she slunk back into the shadows.

"That was no help," Theia said. There would be no murder on her watch (and to be honest, she didn't think there was any on Murdery's, either). Theia was inspired, however, to think outside the box. She hadn't even thought of killing Nerd until now, so her mind was at least open.

One thing they all knew was that their normal life was not a good one. That meant that if they were going to change things, they would have to change the way they lived. Until now, with occasional exceptions, they had been obedient creatures. They followed the rules as they were written for them, though they had no say in the creation of those rules. An idea struck Theia.

"Mittens," Theia called. "Do you know what day it is today?" Ferrets are very good at keeping track of dates.

"It's Monday," Mittens answered. "Why?"

"Animals of the shelter," Theia spoke, addressing them all. "I need everyone to rest tomorrow."

"Why?" Mittens asked again.

"Because tomorrow is Tuesday, and then there's Wednesday," Theia said.

"And what happens on Wednesday?" Mittens dared to ask.

"On Wednesday . . . we riot."

CHAPTER XV

The next morning, Theia began to explain what she understood about the battle between Nerd and Andrea. He reminded them of the other man, Nerd's father, who appeared to have a dominant role within the human pack. Maybe he was in charge in choosing the leader of the shelter, and there was going to be something held to determine who. Theia believed it was going to happen on Wednesday.

"So what can we do?" Mittens asked.

"We have to be bad animals," Theia said. "Show that Nerd has no dominance over us. Bark, meow, hiss, shit, scream."

"I can do that," Sal said, barely disguising her glee.

Andrea walked in, and she was carrying a small cage. In it was a cream-colored guinea pig. There had been another guinea pig or two in the shelter, but they rarely spoke. Theia wasn't sure if they could talk at all.

"Pay attention, Nerd," Andrea said. "This little guy's name is Cheesecake. He's diabetic, so it's kind of a poor taste in name, but he's here to see how the artificial atmosphere affects those with diabetes." She went on to explain that during his feedings, he was to check Cheesecake's blood sugar level. If it was too low, he would have to inject Cheesecake with insulin, which Andrea showed him how to do.

"Okay, got it," Nerd said dismissively.

"I have meetings today," Andrea added, "so I'll need you to drop both reports off tonight after dinner feeding." She took Cheesecake over to an empty cage and placed him inside. She reminded Nerd to keep an eye on him and left the room.

Nerd started the breakfast feeding. Cheesecake was in apparent shock. He had his face pressed against his bars, his eyes slowly panning around the room. The other animals were quite amused.

"Are you okay?" Mittens asked.

"Oh, yeah," Cheesecake said. "I'm peachy. How are you?"

This was already more words than Theia had ever heard a guinea pig utter. Cheesecake had an accent, like the humans on the *Doctor Who* series. The animals found it delightful.

"I'm fine, all things considered," Mittens said. "It's nice to meet you, Cheesecake."

"How'd you know my name?" Cheesecake asked.

"Andrea said it when she brought you in," Mittens said.

"How'd you understand humans?!" Cheesecake asked.

Mittens explained they didn't understand everything, but they did understand tone and a handful of their words.

"Can they understand us?" Cheesecake asked. His eyes darted back and forth.

"Not like they think they can," Sal chimed in.

Nerd distributed the food and then looked into Cheesecake's hutch. He had no interest in injecting this pig with anything, so he made the assumption that Cheesecake was probably fine. He put some food in his dish and shut the door.

"Is he going to give me water?" Cheesecake asked. A water bottle would have had to be found to affix to the empty cage, but since there was no bottle and no extra dish, Nerd forgot entirely about it.

"I'm sure he will," Mittens said, the only animal in the shelter confident of this, and only barely.

Hours passed, and Cheesecake still had no water, and his body was starting to display a different kind of shock from when he arrived. He was shaking, and his bright demeanor had dimmed quite a bit. Theia's attention turned to Nerd, who was napping behind the counter while *E.T.* played in the background.

"We have to get his attention," Theia said to Mittens. "Cheesecake needs water. And maybe the medicine Andrea was talking about. We don't know how long his journey here was."

With that, Theia started to growl. This was to let the other animals know, like a conductor tapping on his stand, that they were to join her choir. Then she started to yip. Other dogs joined in, and then a few cats. Even Randy hissed. Now, they were full on barking as loud as they could, and Nerd abruptly awoke.

"Shut up!" he yelled, and threw a box at the cages. "What is your problem?"

He stood up and turned the sound on the monitor as loud as he could, sat down and turned his back to the animals. They couldn't believe it.

"I'm sorry, Cheesecake," Theia said. The animals sat in their boxes solemnly.

"Theia," Randy hissed.

"What do you want?" she asked.

"I think maybe I can ssssneak out of my cage and open hissss," he said.

"Why?" she asked. "So you can eat him?"

Randy was taken aback. Theia was still remembering her dream about him, feeling that fear again.

"No," Randy said. "Sssso I can help. I make jokessss about eating and hurting you. I have a bad sssssensssse of humor, I'm sssssorry. But I think I can help."

"No, Randy," Theia ordered. "Stay in your cage."

Theia was wondering if her mistrust was misplaced, but she had to trust her gut. Even if Randy could get out, what would he do for Cheesecake?

Another hour passed, and it was time for dinner feeding. Theia got up from a nap, stretched out her front legs and checked up to Cheesecake's cage. He wasn't anywhere to be seen.

"Cheesecake?" Theia called out. "Are you okay?"

Nerd had started dispensing kibble and letting the animals use the metal bathroom box. He got to Theia, and latched her leash onto the pole in the corner. Now that she was closer, she was hoping to have a better look. Cheesecake finally crept out of the shadow, and he appeared to be convulsing. Theia yipped, and Nerd hit her in the nose with the back of his hand without hesitation. Pins and needles shot through Theia's body. He took the leash off the pole and dragged her back to her cage. She barked through the closed door, her bright eyes staring directly at Cheesecake.

Nerd followed her line of sight, and saw him seizing in his pen. He walked over and stared him for a full minute. Cheesecake's limbs were flailing in unnatural directions. He was creating faint squeaks, subtle pleas for help.

Nerd, silently, turned around. He pushed the bathroom box back to its spot. He filled in the evening report, put it on top of the morning report, turned off his computer and monitor, shut off the light and locked the door behind him.

Before he left, Cheesecake had stopped moving.

CHAPTER XVI

Corporal Theremin was unsuccessful in his fight against his discharge. Yeah, he had been caught doing things he shouldn't have, but he had also given over three decades of his life to his country, and he should be allowed to have fun.

Except what he was doing wasn't for fun anymore. He had been using to hide and escape and forget and deflect and rationalize, but he certainly wasn't having fun anymore.

As part of his rehabilitation program, he had been in counseling. Sometimes talking helped, often it didn't. He spoke to someone who was clearly a civilian; she didn't understand his experience in any meaningful way.

When he told her this directly, she took no offense. She hadn't experienced PTSD in any way, shape or form in her life. But in fact, it gave her an idea.

"Some people," she told him, "find comfort and understanding in an animal."

This sounded like some kind of bullshit to him. How could an animal have any idea what he was going through? He liked dogs well enough, had one with his ex-wife, but he wasn't interested in taking care of anyone else. All his counselor asked was for him to have an open mind, and his divorce hadn't happened because he easily compromised in the past. He told her he would at least look.

A week later, he was at a fancy version of an animal shelter. All the animals here, he was told, were specially trained. He reckoned some of the creatures here had more of an education than he had. He wondered if the cats knew math better than he did.

He had to admit he no longer hated the idea. Just a half hour in, petting them, feeding them, feeling a vibe – he started to understand how a support animal system could work. He felt foolish having ever rejected the idea. As he settled in to the idea of bringing one of these friendly beasts home, his eyes caught another's in the corner of the room.

"What's that big guy's story?" he asked.

That big guy was a boa constrictor, trained in the art of compassion. Theremin was smitten. He marched right over and introduced himself. The snake looked him right in the pupil with a level of respect he rarely saw in humans.

He couldn't sign the paperwork fast enough.

Corporal Theremin named his new snake Randy, after his favorite wrestler. He relished in having the kids from the neighborhood stop by, watching their expressions as this fiercely friendly serpent wrapped himself around his trunk and arms. Theremin felt a level of protection that he realized he spent most of his life living without.

For a few months, he made significant progress. His counseling sessions found him more open, more willing to dive into the depths of where he came from. Unfortunately, the darkness in that abyss was deeper than he could swim.

He started using again innocently enough. An old friend stopped by, and it was for old time's sake. That led to using the next day to level himself out. To regular use again.

Randy watched helplessly as Theremin self-destructed before him. Randy was trained, yes, but not for this kind of situation. Neither of them had the tools to get the help they needed, and Theremin's suffering came to an end less than a month after he had gone back to his old ways.

Randy now showed signs of PTSD. They didn't know how to treat that in a snake, but found his behavior fascinating nonetheless.

A needle behind the neck to put him to sleep.

Put up on a shelf by people who didn't know what to do with him.

He felt this pain abruptly as he looked over to the cage Cheesecake was being held in. Cheesecake had been lifeless for minutes now.

He decided to ignore Theia's earlier warnings. His tail wrapped around the latch on his cage and he opened his door. Leaving the large, heavy mass of his body in his crate, he arched his long neck around to Cheesecake's door.

"What are you doing, snake?" Theia scolded. "Leave him alone!"

Randy ignored Theia and opened the pen. He carefully looked inside. Slowly, he pulled his neck out, gently closed the door and returned to his cage,

"I'm ssssorry," he said. "The guinea pig issss not breathing. He issss dead."

This ripped a hole through the shelter. Some of the animals suddenly couldn't breathe. Some of them couldn't believe what had happened, but some of them absolutely could. Theia, for one, saw the signs. She was a sign. She was a perpetual victim of Nerd's.

"The plan remains the same," Theia said, addressing the shelter with a calm voice.

"Tomorrow, we riot. We riot for ourselves, and our rights as animals. We riot for each other, and the bond we all share. We riot for those who can't riot for themselves."

Theia took another look at the quiet cage up above.

"Tomorrow, we riot for Cheesecake."

CHAPTER XVII

The night had been a restless one.

The combination of a murder and the anticipation of the next day had the shelter in a buzz. It was an electric combination of anxiety, grief and anger. All of them were awake before a human showed up. They paced around their boxes.

Theia sniffed the air. It was late. There was already something different about today. About an hour after their normal breakfast feeding time, the door opened, and three humans walked in: Nerd, Andrea and Nerd's father, Neil.

"This will be a simple assessment," Neil said. "This morning, we will have Andrea do the feeding and report, and this evening, Ned will do the same. I will observe both, review my notes and come to a decision as to who should run this shelter. In-between feedings, you two will be interviewed by others on the board and the shelter will remain vacant, as to keep it impartial. Do you understand?"

Both Andrea and Nerd nodded their heads.

"What are they saying?" Sal asked.

"I'm not sure," Theia replied. Andrea started to take out the feeding supplies.

"Don't riot," Theia said. The animals responded dramatically.

"What do you mean?" Mittens asked.

"Be good for Andrea," she said.

"I like being a good dog," Apple said.

"Be like Apple," Theia said.

"But I want to bite!" Sal said.

"I know," Theia said. "I think they're taking turns. Be good for Andrea now, and we riot for Nerd tonight."

"Are you sure?" Sal asked.

"Yes," Theia said, not absolutely sure.

Andrea went through the feeding schedule and the animals obliged. The dogs licked. The cats purred. Even Randy purred. ("Is that snake purring?" Neil asked.)

"Oh, no." Andrea had finally looked into Cheesecake's cage. Her expression became serious. "Nerd, what happened here?"

"What do you mean?" Nerd feigned. The other animals hissed and hollered. "Is there something wrong?"

"You know something's wrong," Andrea said, not fooled. "Cheesecake is dead."

"Look at my report from last night!" Nerd loudly objected. "See! Cheesecake was alive and well!"

"This is unfortunate," Neil said. "We'll have to remove the body and clean that cage."

They did so. Andrea gently wrapped Cheesecake in a blanket and took him out of the shelter. Nerd was more than willing to wash the cage, a murderer getting to clean his own crime scene. The animals were appalled.

When it was finished, Neil spoke to Nerd and Andrea for a little while longer. Theia tried to get the words, but they were quiet. They sounded like commands, or maybe reminders.

They went over to the door, and Andrea took one more look around the shelter. She mouthed the words 'Thank you.' Then the humans turned off the light and left.

"How did we do?" Mittens asked.

"I was so good," Apple said with joy. "I was the goodest."

"Yes, you were, Apple," Theia said. "We all did good, I think."

"But I was the goodest," Apple said.

"Okay, Apple, you were the goodest," Theia relented.

It was hard to decide if they done the right thing, but it felt like the right thing. Andrea was the one they wanted in charge, so it made sense to treat her with kindness and respect, as that was the way she treated them in return.

"We took an unexpected detour this morning, but make no mistake: tonight, we are loud. If Nerd returns, we riot."

Flush from the engagement of the day so far, most of the animals were ready for a nap. They made themselves comfortable, and fell fast asleep.

Theia awoke to a sound. She opened one eye, and saw Nerd sneaking through the door.

What is he up to? she thought.

She stayed down as to not alert him to her awareness. He pulled a small container from his pocket, and started going from one crate to the next, opening and shutting the doors quickly. He got to Theia's crate and opened the door. Her head bolted up quickly by instinct.

"No fooling you, is there?" he said. He closed her door without another word.

He visited a few more cages, returned the container to his pocket and left the shelter as quietly as he entered.

Theia was thoroughly confused. What had just happened? What was in his pocket, and why did he go through the pens?

Having no answers, Theia lied awake and kept asking herself the questions.

Mittens was the first to wake, about an hour after Nerd had stopped by. The other animals gradually joined them, and Theia decided to keep to herself what she had seen until she had an idea why. Telling the animals that they were on the Moon was an eye-opener; they were not going to be easily convinced of anything without objective proof.

They went about their business, cleaning themselves, staying hydrated. Some were quite anxious about the upcoming feeding; some were genuinely looking forward to it. Mittens could tell something was off with Theia.

"You okay, miss?" he asked.

"Yeah," she said. "Actually, something weird happened earlier, and I have to tell somebody about it."

She recounted what occurred during the afternoon to Mittens, not leaving a detail out. He was just as mystified.

"Maybe you should talk to Sal about it," he suggested.

"Sal," Theia whispered across the room. "Sal, I have to talk to you about something."

She wasn't moving.

"Sal!" Theia said loudly, trying to wake her up. "Apple, is Sal okay?"

Apple was busy drinking his water. Theia was irritated and yipped at him.

"Sorry, Theia," Apple said. "Water is real good today."

"What do you mean it's good today, Apple?" Theia asked. "It's water."

"It's sweet," Apple said.

"Is Sal okay?" Theia said.

"Yeah," Apple said, looking over into the cage next to him. "She's just sleeping."

"Try to wake her up," Theia said.

Apple let out a deafening bark. Then he yawned. Sal was barely moving.

"Sal!" Theia yelled again. She was trying to make sense of what could have happened. Then it struck her. She ran over to her water dish and took a drink. It tasted like water.

"Mittens!" she called up. "Taste your water!"

He did as he was told.

"What does it taste like?" she asked.

"It's sweet," he said.

"Don't drink the water!" Theia told the entire shelter. "I don't know what Nerd put in it, but it will make you fall asleep! If your water is sweet, it has been poisoned!"

So that was his trick. He was trying to quell their uprising before it even began. A few of the animals were already out; she hoped that they would up before dinner, and then she would stop them from drinking again.

It was in his cowardly move that Theia realized they had power.

CHAPTER XVIII

"Did I miss it?"

Sal was waking up. She was confused over how she could fall asleep at a time like this. Theia explained everything to her, and she was livid.

"How dare he," she said. She stood up, and it was a slow process. She was in no shape to riot. Apple had only had a few drinks of water before Theia warned them of its poison, and while a few had drunk enough to put them to sleep for a while, they were, for the most part, all awake now.

The door opened, and Andrea, Nerd and Neil walked in. Nerd was astounded. How was it possible that all the animals were awake? If you've ever seen a Boston Terrier, you know they are possible of great smiles; Theia's smile now was unmistakable. It was the smile of a challenger.

Neil gave a similar speech to the one he had that morning. Clear cut, dry and fair, he thought. He reminded them of what was at stake, and then he gave Nerd permission to start the evening feeding.

Nerd dragged out the metal box for bathroom use. It screeched against the floor, and made an immediate impression on his father. He apologized, and started for the pens.

The first cell he came up to was Sal's. Poor Sal was in feeble shape. She could barely keep her eyes open, and it was hard for the other animals to watch. He swung open her door and filled her dish with food. Noticing the lack of fight in her eyes, he realized she must have ingested some of the drug. He took advantage of the moment and gave Sal a rub behind her cheeks. Theia growled.

"This one has a particular soft spot for me," Nerd said. Andrea could immediately sense something wasn't right. Neil looked pleasantly surprised. Nerd put the leash on Sal's collar and pulled on her to leave the crate.

She wouldn't budge.

Sal was putting all her weight down, refusing to come out. The others lit up. Andrea was smiling, too. Nerd pulled and pulled, but she was immovable, even as her gold collar squeezed up under her throat.

Then, Sal stood up. Nerd looked relieved. Without breaking eye contact with him, Sal then took the biggest shit Theia had ever seen. Now Sal was relieved.

Neil wrote down some notes, shaking his head incredulously. Nerd shoved his hand in her collar again, pulling her out the crate and into the bathroom box.

"Hey!" Andrea called, but Neil asked her to stay silent during the assessment. Apple was starting to sweat, knowing he was next.

"I don't want to be a bad dog," he was repeating to himself. Theia recognized his anxiety.

"Then play," she said. "Play with Nerd, but don't stop when he tells you to."

"Play?" Apple asked. "I can play."

Sal was put back into her cage, just cleaned by Nerd, and he moved onto Apple's crate. He barely moved the latch on the door when Apple came barreling through, pushing Nerd onto his back and jumping on top of his chest. He started barking loudly and without any foreseeable end. He then galloped around the shelter, the other animals cheering him on. Watching him proudly bound around the room, his golden locks bouncing from side to side, was an unmistakable moment of joy for the lot. As Apple made eye contact with Theia, a leash snapped onto his collar and he was led to the bathroom box. Apple had done good.

Two more dogs followed. They growled and barked and made a scene from the moment he opened their doors to when they were closed.

"Good job, everybody," Theia encouraged them.

He came to Murdery's cage, and Murdery did nothing but lick his hairless paw while Nerd filled up his dish and let him use the bathroom.

"Boo, Murdery!" Theia said.

"Murdery sucks!" Sal added.

Mittens was next. When Nerd got to his crate, he was nowhere to be found.

"Did the ferret escape again?" Neil asked.

"No. He was here this afternoon," Nerd said, realizing that was possibly too much. He opened the door and traced the box with his hand. Terrifically, Mittens jumped out of hiding under his blanket and jumped onto Nerd's face. Nerd took four big steps backwards, then tripped over the bathroom box and landed on his back in the middle of it.

This got an uproarious reaction from the rest of the shelter.

Mittens then ran around him, eventually running over to Andrea and crawling up to her shoulder. Andrea did everything she could to only smile patiently. She placed Mittens back in his crate and shut the door, returning to her position next to Neil.

Nerd stood up, trying to remain cool and calm, while looking like a steamed tomato. He reluctantly went to the next crates, receiving the same unruly behavior, again and again. He was clearly reaching the end of his patience.

He got to Randy. Theia had no idea what was going to happen next. He opened Randy's door and flinched a little, but Randy remained still. He fed Randy a cold mouse, and as Randy swallowed it, he extended himself down Nerd's arm. He wound himself all the way around Nerd's neck; he looked over to find his father looking impressed, so he let the boa do its thing.

Randy, now wrapped around both of Nerd's arms and his neck, looked at him right in the eyes and slowly did what he was known for doing: constricting. The red in Nerd's face amplified, his breath decreased and he was holding his bowels tight inside. Randy squeezed until he heard simple pops; just a little crack of the back was needed to show him who was really in control.

Then Randy, just as slowly as he came on, slithered off Nerd's body and back into his box. The other animals had been holding their own breath this entire time, and now let out a collective sigh. Theia respected this move greatly; she felt bad for having judged Randy the way she did, especially after he had tried to apologize and help.

The only cage left was Theia's. Nerd looked like he had just run a marathon through the desert while it rained poop from the sky. He looked sad and ridiculous, and a small part of her pitied him, but only because they were both animals.

He looked at her intently, and hesitantly unlatched her door. She walked with confidence right up to his face, and licked him right on the lips.

He was taken aback. Was this some kind of trick? She put her front paws up on his legs, inviting him to pet her. He turned around to Andrea and his father, his face unable to hide the confusion he was feeling. And while he was turned looking at them, Theia spread her hind legs and peed on his shoes.

He wasn't surprised by this immediate betrayal. So he just let her finish up, dumped her kibble in the dish and shut the door. He pulled the metal box back to its spot against the wall and put the rest of the feeding supplies away. He joined Andrea and his father, who had been chatting. Andrea looked upset.

"What's up?" he asked.

"We both heard what you said about the ferret," Neil told him. "You mentioned that he had been here this afternoon, and you shouldn't have been."

"What does that mean?" Nerd asked.

"I told Andrea I think the assessment has been compromised, and we should reschedule another," Neil said. "In the meantime, you would be allowed to keep your position and work on your . . . relationship with the animals."

Theia could see the look in Andrea's eyes. They had failed.

No, no, no.

She could feel their chance slipping away, when she realized something. Maybe Randy didn't represent her fear in the dream. No, Randy was the rope pulling her in. It was up to him, she knew it.

"Randy," she said. "Get us out of here."

"What?" he asked.

"Get yourself out," Theia directed, "Mittens, you, too. Then both of you let as many of us out as you can. We need to show them who we pick."

Randy didn't need a second thought. He broke free and started unlatching all the doors he could reach. Mittens dropped down in front of Theia's cage and let her out. They ran to the other side and got Sal and Apple and the rest.

"Follow me!" Theia said.

The humans had noticed the commotion by this time. All the freed animals were running as one pack towards them. Nerd jumped behind the counter, covering himself with his arms. He heard some laughter, and then peeked his head back over the counter.

The animals had surrounded Andrea. They were wrapped around her, licking, pawing, purring. Theia made eye contact with Neil, her bright eyes telling him clearly that this was their choice, and she was their choice.

Neil looked them over and it was unanimous.

"This is your zoo now," he said.

CHAPTER XIX

Not that the zoo started running smoothly on day one.

Nerd contested the demotion for weeks. He would show up at the shelter before Andrea some mornings, until they changed the locks and he was ordered to stay away. She kept Nerd's films on the monitor, and this pleased Theia to no end.

At first, Andrea was unsure of herself. She knew that she cared about the animals, and that was the most important part. But how could she make things better? That was something that took time and a lot of thought.

She started rewarding behavior, which was a new concept to the animals. They had already committed to being kind to one another, but to get gifts for their kindness was not unappreciated, and it somehow made even Apple a gooder dog.

She let them out at all feeding times, not just dinner. And there were no leashes involved. They were already in this room together; there was no reason for more control than was necessary. They were allowed to sniff and walk and lay and be animals.

The best thing that Andrea implemented, though, was playtime. Every day, right in the middle of it, she opened all the crate doors of the shelter and let whoever wanted come out and play together. To make it even more magical, she started inviting the other humans who lived at the base over to play with them, too. They made so many new friends, and the idea of loneliness felt more like an echo each day.

The shelter didn't feel like a dead end anymore, because it was made into a home. They were learning new things daily, about their world and each other, and it made the abstract things Theia used to run towards feel like empty fields.

"Do you ever miss your home?" Mittens asked.

"Of course," Theia said.

"What do you miss about it?" he asked.

"I miss the feeling of love I had there," she said. "I guess I just missed the idea. Because I used that idea to bring my love here, and now I don't miss it nearly as much."

"That's nice," Mittens said.

"It is," Theia agreed.

CHAPTER XX

Within a few months of Andrea running the shelter, it was more full than it had ever been. Animals were coming in from all over the planet, and they were being brought into a community that was kind and understanding and supportive. It was a chaotic time, and Mittens thought it would be good during a playtime if Theia would welcome them all and tell them a story.

So Theia did.

She told them the story of a dog. All the dog wanted to do was go outside. But when she asked herself why, she never had an answer.

The dog, not sure of why it wanted to escape, then dug, fought, clawed, chewed and ran towards an idea, at the expense of herself and those who cared about her.

She ignored all common sense, wisdom and her own instincts to get there, and when her idea of there began to fade, she had wondered why she had been so stubborn in the first place.

She had to become humble. She had to say she was sorry. She had to return everything she had stolen but not yet spent.

It was hard.

She had to learn how to serve. She had to learn compassion and empathy. She had to give everything she could and then a little more.

That was easier.

Mittens, of course, knew this story was about Theia, as did a few of the other, sharper animals (Apple did not get it). But Mittens's version of the story was much shorter.

Theia was once a dog who just wanted to go outside.

Then Theia was the dog who learned how to stay.

The End

Also by Dennis Vogen

<u>Novellas</u>

Them

Us

Flip

<u>Graphic Novels</u>

The Weirdos: Volume I

www.ingramcontent.com/pod-product-compliance
Lightning Source LLC
Chambersburg PA
CBHW050350030726
47503CB00008B/2709